T0018812

I like the RAIN

written by Sarah Nelson • illustrated by Rachel Oldfield

Barefoot Books
step inside a story

I like the rain —

pitter-patting through the green,
washing all the petals clean,

tapping on my nose and cheeks.
This is how the rain speaks.

I like the rain —

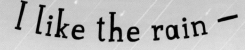

falling, falling down in sheets
in cool, refreshing, silver streaks.

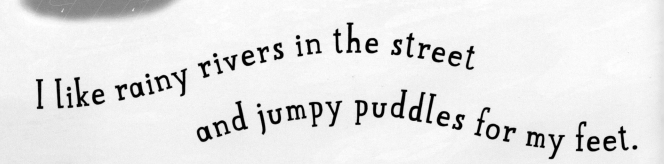

I like rainy rivers in the street
and jumpy puddles for my feet.

I like splattering and splashing!
I like running, leaping, laughing!

As roly-rumbly skies are coming,
I like distant storm clouds drumming.

Bolts of lightning, flishing-flashing!
Booming, bashing thunder crashing!

Peeking out from under cushions,

watching rainy, rushing oceans.

I like it, too, when storm clouds pass
and sunlight beams in through the glass.

Then through a million drops of rain,
the sunlight paints its rainbow stain

on white, wet clouds.

I like the rain.

Questions for a Rainy Day

Where does rain come from?

Rain is recycled water. It comes from our oceans, lakes and rivers. When sunlight warms these bodies of water, some of the water changes from a liquid into a gas (which we cannot see!) and rises up into the air. In the sky, this gas cools into extremely tiny drops of water, called droplets, and forms clouds. The water droplets bounce around, cling together and grow bigger. In time, the water droplets become too heavy for the air to hold. Then they fall to Earth as raindrops. Eventually, rain water flows back into rivers, lakes and oceans. This movement of water, which is always happening, is called the water cycle.

Why do rainbows appear?

Rainbows can appear as rain clouds move away and the sun peeks through. Sunlight is a mixture of the whole rainbow — red, orange, yellow, green, blue, indigo and violet. When sunlight passes through raindrops at just the right angle, the light bends and separates into rainbow stripes.

What are lightning and thunder?

Lightning is a flash of electricity released from a storm cloud. During powerful storms, droplets of water and bits of ice are tossed up and down through the clouds. These tiny water droplets and bits of ice crash into one another, which makes electricity. When enough electricity builds up, it moves to the ground or to another cloud, creating a bright flash of lightning. The lightning suddenly heats and expands the air it touches. This produces a loud boom or rumble, called thunder. Thunder is noisy, but it can't hurt us. Lightning, however, can be dangerous. When you hear thunder or see lightning, it's time to head indoors.

How does rain help us?

Rain keeps the planet green and growing. All plants and animals, from dandelions to elephants, need fresh water in order to live. Rain provides that water to us in almost every place on Earth. Rain waters our food crops, fills lakes and rivers, replenishes our drinking wells and cools and cleans us on a hot, dusty day. Thank you, rain!

Enjoy more weather fun with *I Like the Sun*, *I Like the Wind* and *I Like the Snow*.

For Tom, who used to stomp in rain puddles with me — S. N.

For Pat and Malcolm, for all that you bring — R. O.

Barefoot Books
2067 Massachusetts Ave
Cambridge, MA 02140

Barefoot Books
29/30 Fitzroy Square
London, W1T 6LQ

Text copyright © 2021 by Sarah Nelson
Illustrations copyright © 2021 by Rachel Oldfield
The moral rights of Sarah Nelson and Rachel Oldfield have been asserted

First published in United States of America by Barefoot Books, Inc
and in Great Britain by Barefoot Books, Ltd in 2021. All rights reserved

Graphic design by Elizabeth Kaleko, Barefoot Books
Edited and art directed by Kate DePalma, Barefoot Books
Reproduction by Bright Arts, Hong Kong

Printed in China on 100% acid-free paper
This book was typeset in Century Gothic, Cut-Out,
Dear St. Nick and Mr Lucky
The illustrations were prepared in acrylics

Hardback ISBN 978-1-64686-098-2 • E-book ISBN 978-1-64686-016-6

British Cataloguing-in-Publication Data:
a catalogue record for this book is available from the British Library

Library of Congress Cataloging-in-Publication Data
is available under LCCN 2020009334

3 5 7 9 8 6 4 2

Barefoot Books
step inside a story

At Barefoot Books, we celebrate art and story that opens the hearts and minds of children from all walks of life, focusing on themes that encourage independence of spirit, enthusiasm for learning and respect for the world's diversity. The welfare of our children is dependent on the welfare of the planet, so we source paper from sustainably managed forests and constantly strive to reduce our environmental impact. Playful, beautiful and created to last a lifetime, our products combine the best of the present with the best of the past to educate our children as the caretakers of tomorrow.

www.barefootbooks.com

Sarah Nelson

lives with her husband in Minnesota, USA, where she likes walking barefoot in the rain. Sarah is also a teacher and the author of several books for young children, including *Frogness*. Learn more about Sarah and her books at sarahnelsonbooks.com.

Rachel Oldfield

lives with her husband, three sons and three cats in England, where she teaches illustration at the University of Gloucestershire. She can also be found taking her horse Billy for walks along the country lanes. In addition to the I Like the Weather series, Rachel has illustrated *Up, Up, Up!* and *Outdoor Opposites* for Barefoot Books.